Munching Lunch

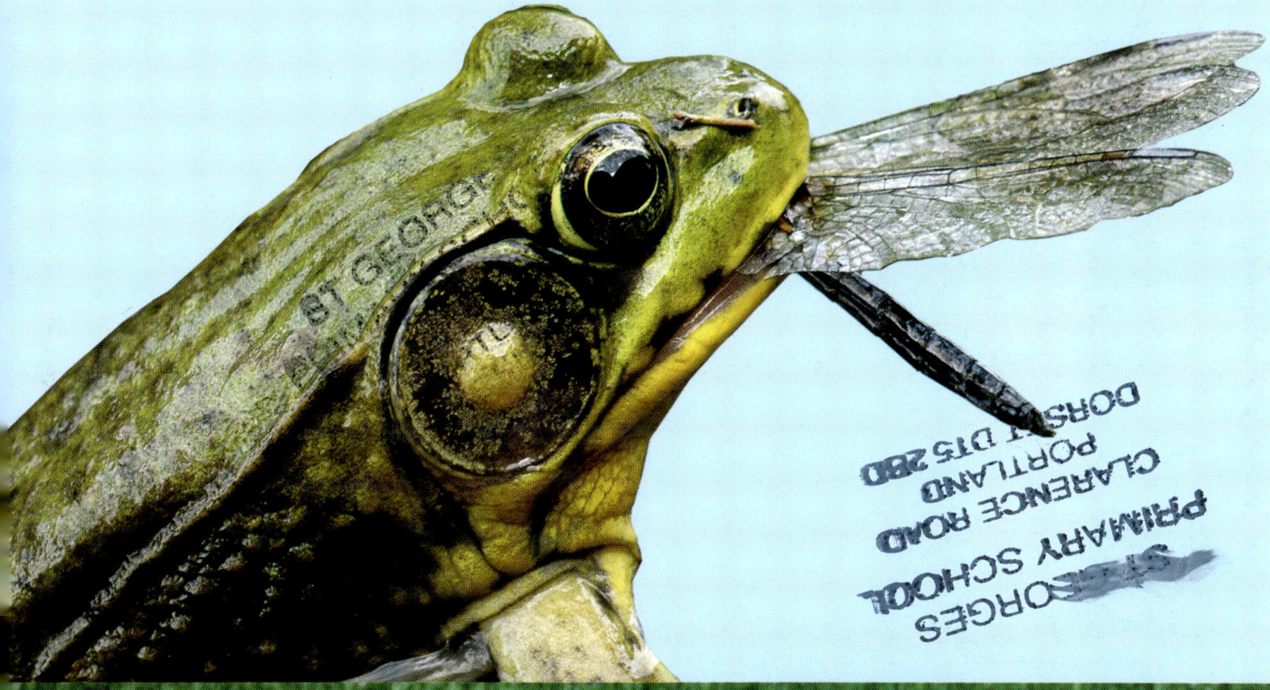

Written by Emma Lynch

The big cat hunts a zebra.

Will she get it?

This gull is hunting.

It has got the fish.

The frog sits on a log ...

then it munches a bug.

Mum and cubs go hunting.

The cubs sit and Mum hunts.

She will get the cubs a big fish.

The chimp can bash a nut's shell with a stick.

This chimp jabs a nest of bugs.

She munches the bugs on the stick.

Camels can munch shrubs ...

and sticks.

They can munch lots of things!